Spooks and Scares!

Look out for more stories
about Disastrous Dez!

Mischief and Mayhem!

Spooks and Scares!

Mary Hooper

illustrated by Judy Brown

■SCHOLASTIC

Scholastic Children's Books,
Commonwealth House, 1-19 New Oxford Street,
London, WC1A 1NU, UK
a division of Scholastic Ltd
London ~ New York ~ Toronto ~ Sydney ~ Auckland
Mexico City ~ New Delhi ~ Hong Kong

First published by Scholastic Ltd, 2002

Text copyright © Mary Hooper, 2002
Illustrations copyright © Judy Brown, 2002

ISBN 0 439 98181 6

Printed and bound in Great Britain by Cox & Wyman Ltd, Reading, Berkshire

2 4 6 8 10 9 7 5 3 1

Chapter One

"Whoooo…" I moaned spookily under my breath in class. "Whooo…"

I'd been practising ghost noises at home for ages, and now I could do them without moving my lips at all. "Whooo … whooo…" No one would know that it was me.

"Yes, thank you, Dez," Miss Brown said. "Less of the animal noises please."

"It wasn't animals – it was ghosts!" I said indignantly. I turned to my friend James. "It was a ghost, wasn't it? Didn't it sound like a ghost?"

Before he could say anything to back me up, Miss Brown walked up to our table. "I hope, Dez," she said, "that this doesn't mean you're going to be naughty on this trip to Graveney Hall. I hope I'm not going to regret allowing you to come. Because I can remember a certain trip to a waxworks last year, and the way you changed two people's heads round…"

"No, I'm going to be really good, Miss!" I said quickly. "Honest!"

"I do hope so," said Miss Brown. She went back to the front of the class.

"Will we really see ghosts at Graveney Hall?" Sasha asked.

"I can't promise that," Miss Brown said, "but you can be sure if there *is* anything spooky going on, then we'll find out about it."

Everyone in our class – even bully-boy Derek Dobbs – turned and grinned at each other. We were really excited. We'd been excited for about four months, actually, ever since Miss Brown had told us that we'd been chosen to go on a special trip to a big house which was supposed to be haunted. People with special ghost-detecting equipment were coming from London and, best of all, we'd be staying there all night!

Ghost-hunting isn't a thing we normally do at school, but Miss Brown said the trip was part of our science class and part of our history class. We weren't going there to mess around, she kept telling us, we had to observe the scientific equipment, make charts, write it up afterwards and be very sensible indeed.

"I've chosen this class because I think you – most of you – know how to behave," she said. "Last year my chosen class went to a museum to stay overnight and they behaved beautifully."

While she was speaking I was tickling my nose with a feather. We'd started doing this at school a couple of weeks ago to see how many times we could sneeze without stopping – so far Sasha had the record at seventeen sneezes and I was hoping to beat it.

"Dez!" Miss Brown suddenly shouted. "Beautiful behaviour. This means everyone, and especially you!"

I dropped the feather and tried to look beautifully behaved and very sensible indeed – we all did – but then it went a bit wrong because Derek Dobbs stuck a caterpillar on Melanie's head and she screamed and screamed and a small fight broke out at the back of the class.

Miss Brown broke it up, telling Derek Dobbs that if he started being silly on the trip he'd be sent straight home, and that anyone (she was looking at me again) who showed off or was naughty would never go on another trip ever again.

"There's just one more thing," she said as the bell went. "I've written letters to your parents listing everything you'll need to bring, and I've mentioned that we haven't got quite enough helpers. I need some of you to persuade your mums and dads to come along too."

We all just looked at her, and then looked at each other and made faces. No one wanted their mum and dad there. As if!

"If Mum or Dad is willing to come, perhaps they could send a note back with you in the morning." She clapped her hands. "So if I don't see you tomorrow, I'll see you all here at school at seven o'clock on Saturday night, ready to catch the coach!"

We took our letters as we went out, then went into huddles, trying to outdo each other about the things we were going to see at Graveney Hall.

"I think there'll be things that go bump in the night," Melanie said.

We all looked at her in disgust. "It'll be much scarier than that," James said. "There'll be ghouls with their heads under their arms."

"Taps dripping blood!" said Sasha.

"Headless horsemen!" said Dee.

"Blood-sucking phantom creatures from the black lagoon coming up out of graves with their heads chopped off carrying them on spikes in front of them!" I said.

They all looked at me.

"Well, really bad things, anyway," I said.

Chapter Two

I don't believe in ghosts. Not really. At school when we were all pretending we were going to see headless horsemen and monks floating out of windows I pretended as well – but I didn't really think we'd see them.

I don't believe in ghosts because for the last four Halloweens I've stayed awake especially to see one, but never have.

Last year I even left a note on my door to encourage them. It read: GHOSTS AND OTHER SPOOKY THINGS THIS WAY, but nothing came.

So I wasn't excited about going to Graveney Hall because of the ghosts, but because of being up till really, really late, because of having a midnight feast and – best of all – because it was going to be a laugh. It would be like having a big sleepover party, same as the girls in our class have.

After school I went to Mrs-Keynes-down-the-road to wait for Dad to get home from work, and at six o'clock he came to call for me.

As he rang the bell Mrs Keynes was just telling me that she positively didn't have another single biscuit of any description in the house. She murmured something like, "Such a relief to hear that bell go..." so I think it may have been broken and she'd just got it fixed.

Dad had two bundles of fish and chips under his arm and we ran up the road to eat them before they got cold. I switched on the telly and we sat down and then unrolled the newspapers.

"Want a plate?" Dad said.

I shook my head.

"Knife and fork?"

I shook it again. "Why? Is Gran coming?" I asked.

Dad grinned. It was one of our jokes: we only ate at the table properly if Granny was coming to visit.

I sprinkled vinegar all over my chips (and a bit over the carpet) and handed the bottle to Dad. "I've got the list of stuff I'm meant to have on my trip," I said.

"Jolly good. I mean, cool," Dad said. Sad, really. He thinks he's being trendy when he uses words like that.

"I've got a sleeping bag, haven't I? And a pillow. And warm clothes and a torch – oh, and I've got to take something to eat for the midnight feast."

"What sort of something?"

I shrugged. "Dunno. Sasha's mum's cooking some brownies. James is bringing sandwiches and Dee's bringing twelve bags of crisps."

"Carrots, then," Dad said. "Carrots are good!"

I shot a quick look to see if he was joking. Unfortunately he wasn't.

"But everyone else is bringing nice things," I said. "Cakes and stuff."

"Carrots are nice. Carrots help you see in the dark... How d'you know?" Dad asked. "Well, have you ever seen a rabbit with glasses?"

I didn't bother to reply to this. I'd heard it at least 400 times before.

With my free hand I pulled the list out of my pocket. "Here's the list. If you've got binoculars you have to take them, and a camera, and anyone who wears glasses has to have a spare pair, and if they take any pills..."

"Show me," Dad said, and I passed the list over.

"It says here that they're short of helpers," he said after a moment. "They want a few mums and dads to come along."

Eeek! I'd forgotten about the bit on the bottom of the note. "Oh ... er ... I think they've got enough people now," I said quickly.

"Have they, Dez...?" Dad said in his I-think-we're-fibbing voice.

"But you don't want to come!" I said. "I thought you were going out with Alex from work on Saturday. I thought you were going to be pleased to see the back of me – that's what you said."

"I was joking!" Dad said. "Besides, Alex is off sick." He looked at the letter again. "Which teachers are going?"

"Not sure. Miss Brown and Miss..."

"Miss Brown!" Dad sat upright suddenly and a piece of fish dropped on to the floor. "Is Miss Brown the one with short blonde hair? The pretty one with big eyes and pink-framed glasses? The one who wears leather trousers?" He grinned. "Not that I've really noticed her..."

I stared at Dad. Don't tell me he fancied Miss Brown! He was a sad case all right.

"I think she's got glasses..." I said. I tried to sound as off-putting as possible. "But honestly, they don't need anyone else now. They've got all the helpers they want."

"That's what you tell me," he said. He stuffed a big piece of batter into his mouth and reached for a pen. "I'll just write a few words on the back of this letter and you can take it in tomorrow. If they've got enough helpers, then that's okay. But if she wants anyone else, then I'm her man!"

"Right," I said.

The letter, of course, didn't have to get to her. In fact, I was going to make sure it didn't.

Chapter Three

"Well, well, well!" Dad said as we waited
for the coach to turn up at school on
Saturday evening. Then he laughed and
said, "Three holes in the ground! Geddit?"

"Yes, Dad," I said. "I always get it."

He rubbed his hands and looked round.
"Where's Miss Brown, then?"

"I don't know," I said. "Perhaps she's not
coming. It's not too late to change your
mind, you know."

"Change my mind?! Not on your nelly!"

I sighed. The very worst thing had happened: Dad was coming on the trip. He was an extra dad. I hadn't given in the note, I'd "accidentally" left it at home, but he'd found it and phoned up Miss Brown at school to offer his services. Of course – well, this is what *Dad* said – Miss Brown was thrilled at the thought of having an extra man around. "Just in case the going gets tough," he'd bragged to me.

I looked at him now. He was wearing a new navy blue tracksuit with a bright red T-shirt underneath, like he was Superman or something. He'd got gel in his hair and he smelled ... I sniffed and shuddered, "You've got that aftershave on, haven't you?" I said. "You smell like a hyena."

He just smirked. "Miss Brown might like hyenas."

I groaned. "I hope you're not going to show me up."

"*Me* show *you* up? That'd make a change!" He gave me a wink. "I think she remembered me from parents' night. She told me she'd be specially pleased to have me around."

As I said: sad.

The coach arrived and we climbed aboard. I left Dad and sat at the back with Sasha. I was going to try and pretend he didn't belong to me.

"Got all your stuff with you?" Sasha asked. "Got everything on the list?"

I nodded and held up my rucksack. "And some extra things," I said. I lowered my voice. "Secret stuff."

"What sort of secret stuff?" whispered Sasha.

"You'll see," I said. "I've spent some of my birthday money," I added, and winked at her. I couldn't wait to try them out.

This is what I'd brought:

1. Spiders' web stuff, like you put on the Christmas tree.
2. Horrid and ghoulish Halloween mask.
3. Tub of green slime.
4. Owl hoot whistle.
5. White handkerchief and some cotton.

Graveney Hall was about sixty kilometres away. I'd been there once, years ago, and could just remember a tall old building with twisted chimneys and windows with coloured glass.

It had had a moat around it and loads of suits of armour in the hall – which wasn't like a hall you'd get at home, but called a Great Hall. The hall had big old furniture in it, flags hanging from the ceiling, and stags' heads stuck all over the walls.

When we arrived they were all ready for us. The ghost hunters from London had already arrived – there was Dave (a weirdy-beardy), Simon (trendy glasses) and Lucy (dark hair right down her back). They were busy setting up what they called their Electronic Detection Equipment in different places around the Great Hall. We went to talk to them each in turn, and asked questions, and then we wrote the answers in our notebooks.

There were three machines.
One that measured
if the temperature
fell suddenly
in a room.

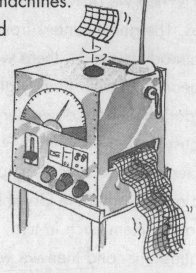

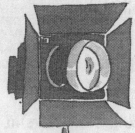

A special camera that
took pictures of spooks
even in total darkness.

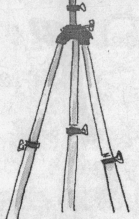

A sound recorder,
to record even
tiny weeny
ghostly sounds.

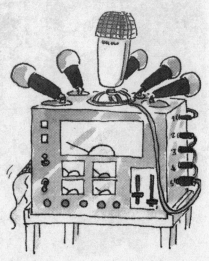

"Are you a ghost hunter?" I asked Lucy. "Like on *Scooby-Doo*?"

She laughed. "We're actually called psychic investigators," she said, "and we come to places like Graveney Hall, where ghosts have been seen, to take readings and to see if we can detect anything unusual."

"What ghosts have been seen here?" James asked.

"Well, over the years there have been several sightings of an old servant carrying a glass of wine ...

and some of
a ghost bride ...

and some people say they've seen the ghost
of a knight in armour
striding across
the gallery
above us.

The sound of a carriage and horses clip-
clopping down the drive has been heard, too."

"And why have you got the temperature thing?" Sasha asked.

"Well, people who've seen apparitions always say that it gets very cold just before the ghost appears," Dave said. "This machine will record that drop in temperature."

"We also have non-scientific things with us," Simon added. "For example, sometimes we sprinkle talcum powder across the floor. Humans leave footprints – ghosts don't!"

Dad cleared his throat and I sort of shrank down a little. He was going to say something embarrassing, I knew it.

"So with you lot, those spooks won't stand a ghost of a chance!"
he said, and the
rest of the class,
including
Miss Brown,
laughed.
I didn't.

Chapter Four

"Now, before we eat, let's decide on our sleeping arrangements," Miss Brown said. "I suggest the adults take a turn each on watch throughout the night. I think it's unrealistic to expect a child to stay awake."

"I don't mind!" I said eagerly, thinking that would make it all the easier to put certain spooky plans into action.

"No," Miss Brown said firmly. "We'll just have one adult on watch, and they can change over every two hours."

"Let me take the first watch," Dad said. "I never sleep before two in the morning anyway." He said this in a macho way, as if he was out fighting bears every night at this time.

"That would be kind of you," Miss Brown said, and Dad beamed at her and wafted a bit more aftershave her way.

"Now, we're going to split up into three groups for sleeping," she went on. "You can choose to sleep under the gallery, in the recess next to the stairs, or in that alcove by the front door."

"I want to be under the gallery!" I said quickly, and added to Sasha, "If I'm going to see something, I want to see the knight in armour. A proper ghost. Not an old servant or a silly bride."

"I want to see the bride," Sasha said.

"I don't care what I see," James said. "I just want to see something spooky."

Well, he would certainly do that, I thought...

34

It was midnight feast time (well, it was actually ten o'clock but we couldn't wait any longer) and it was looking pretty spooky in the Great Hall. A thick paper cover had been put along the long wooden table which ran down the middle, and the teachers had lit the candles in the big iron holders and turned all the lights off.

Everyone started getting their food from their bags to put on the table. They brought out their fun-size choc bars, crisps, fruit cake and brownies, and I didn't bring out anything.

"Where's your food, then?" James asked.

"I … er … forgot to put it in," I said. "I had some great big jam doughnuts and I completely forgot 'em."

"Doughnuts?" Dad said. "No, not doughnuts, Dez. Carrots!"

I frowned at him. "Yeah, well I forgot those as well."

"No, you didn't!" Dad said. "I put them in the bag myself. Look again, Dez – we want to have our carrots, don't we, because..."

"I'm looking!" I interrupted, scrabbling in the bag. "I'm looking, and they're not there."

"Pass the bag over," Dad said, and then he grabbed it from me and fished out the carrots. "Here we are! I knew we had them!"

"Carrots!" James said, surprise in his voice.
We slid on to the wooden benches on
each side of the table, and Dad put the
carrots into one of the big wooden bowls.

"Carrots!" Miss Brown said. "That's
certainly different." I saw her looking at one
of the mum-helpers and raising her eyebrows.

"I thought they'd come in handy," Dad said.

"You know they say that carrots can help you see in the dark." He smiled around him, "Well, I bet you've never seen a rab—"

Drastic measures were called for. I pointed towards one of the long windows in the hall. "Aaarrgghhh!" I yelled. "There's a horrible face looking in at us!"

It did look quite horrible, actually. The face was a shiny luminous green. It had its mouth open in a never-ending moan and a strange unearthly glow came from its eyes.

Everyone jumped, some of the girls screamed and Derek Dobbs got under the table. Dad didn't even finish the word "rabbit" – he just went all white and drew in his breath in a big gasp.

The teachers jumped to their feet. "What on earth is that?" Miss Brown said.

Dave the ghost hunter went across to the window. "I think you'll find it's just someone having a joke," he said, picking up my mask. "It's a ghoul mask from Halloween, and it's been placed on the window with a torch behind it." He smiled, "It's a good trick – you'd hardly notice it when the hall lights were on, but now they're off it looks quite alarming."

Dad sidled over to me and spoke in a low voice. "Is that your torch and mask?"

I looked at it, blinked several times and then nodded. "I think it is," I said. "Someone must have stolen them out of my bag."

"Is that so?" Dad said sternly. "We'll talk about this later, Dez."

"Are you feeling all right?" I asked. "You've gone a funny colour. You didn't really think it was the face of a ghastly ghoul, did you?"

"Don't be ridiculous," Dad said. "I knew it was a mask straight away." He gave a great bellow of laughter, making Miss Brown jump. "Oh, it would take a good deal more than that to fool me, Dez. I'm not known as Frank the Fearless for nothing."

"I didn't know you were anyway," I said as I got on with scoffing everyone else's food.

Chapter Five

By eleven thirty we were all in our sleeping
bags in our spook-selected places. I was
under the gallery, ready to see the knight,
and Dad was on one side of me and James
on the other. One of the other teachers had
read a long ghost story which hadn't been
very scary, and then everyone had started
yawning and yawning.

"Well, it's been a long night," Miss Brown said. "I think we might just as well try to sleep."

Soon as we snuggled down, though, everyone seemed to miraculously come awake again.

"I'm not going to sleep anyway," I said to James. "I'm going to stay awake every minute of the night. I'm not going to miss a thing."

Every fifteen minutes, one of the ghost hunter people trundled over to check a piece of the equipment, then came back shaking their head and saying there was nothing to report. James fell asleep quite quickly and it was getting boring, so I decided it was time to spook things up a bit.

I crawled right down into my sleeping bag so no one could see me and started making owl hoots with my special owl hoot whistle – low, spooky owl cries in the darkness.

I didn't think anyone would realize it was me, but when I came up for air, Dad and Miss Brown were standing by my sleeping bag, looking cross.

"No more of that, please, Dez," Miss Brown said. Dad gave me a glowering look and said he would personally throw me to the lions if there was any more mucking about.

Rather miffed at being detected, I let another ten minutes go by, then worked out my next plan and slid out of my sleeping bag, pretending I wanted to go to the loo. This was a five minute walk down a murky old corridor. The mum on loo duty had to come with me, but on our way back into the hall I got rid of her by giving a great shiver.

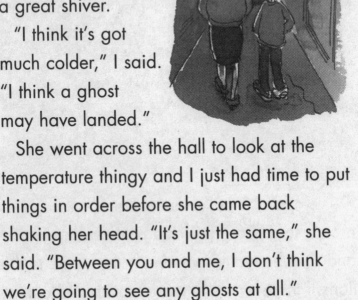

"I think it's got much colder," I said. "I think a ghost may have landed."

She went across the hall to look at the temperature thingy and I just had time to put things in order before she came back shaking her head. "It's just the same," she said. "Between you and me, I don't think we're going to see any ghosts at all."

"Oh, we might," I said, then added politely, "Thank you for taking me," and got back into my sleeping bag.

Ten minutes later it had gone quiet all round the room apart from Dad and one or two others snoring. Snoring – and Dad was supposed to be on watch!

I pulled on the long piece of cotton that, on my loo run, I'd managed to attach to the middle of a white hanky and twist round the highest banister I could reach on the stairs. The hanky, which I'd hidden at the foot of the last stair, rose into the air, looking just like a little wispy ghost.

As I tugged and then loosened the cotton, it rose and fell, fluttering spookily. Brilliant, it was.

Automatically, the special camera started clicking – which immediately alerted the ghost hunters and Miss Brown. Suddenly four torches were shining on my little ghost and everyone who wasn't fast asleep sat up and made noises of fright or surprise.

I gave one last pull on my piece of cotton and then let it drop. My ghost fell to the floor – just as Simon the ghost hunter rushed over to it.

"It's a handkerchief!" he said. "A hanky and a long piece of cotton."

"Wassat? Who … what?" Dad said, sitting up in his sleeping bag. "What's going on?"

"Another trick," said Miss Brown. She got out of her sleeping bag next to the stairs and came very close to where I was sleeping. And I *was* sleeping, of course, eyes tight shut and snoring gently.

"I'm not sure," I heard her say to Dad, "but I wouldn't be at all surprised if that wasn't another of Dez's so-called jokes."

"Surely not," Dad said.

"Perhaps if you could just watch him a little more closely, Mr Williams," Miss Brown said in a low voice. "I've been relying on you for that – that's why I was so grateful when I heard you were coming."

"Call me Frank," said Dad.

"Only it must be rather annoying for the psychic researchers to have someone play tricks on them."

There was a moment's silence and I knew they were both looking closely at me, so I did a couple of twitches and snorts in my sleep.

Miss Brown walked away – I could hear her leather trousers creaking – and Dad poked me in the shoulder. "I know that was you and I know you're awake," he hissed. "Apart from anything else, you're spoiling my chances with Miss Brown, you little beast!"

I stirred a little. "Wassat?" I muttered. "What did you say?" I opened my eyes and looked at him blearily. "I've been fast asleep."

"Oh, sure you have," Dad said.

Chapter Six

After that I tried to get to sleep for hours, but just couldn't. I tried and I tried but it was so strange sleeping on the floor in a sleeping bag in that great big place, and every time I turned round I kept knotting myself up. Hours went by and Dad was asleep, Miss Brown was asleep – I think even the ghost hunters were asleep.

I reached over to my rucksack and searched around for the spooky cobweb stuff. I decided to put it all over Dad's head so that if he woke in the night he'd find himself trussed up like a Christmas tree. That would be really funny.

Slowly, I edged the rucksack closer, got out the cardboard box and began to pull out the grey cobwebs inside. Getting a great handful of them, I turned round and shuffled along in my sleeping bag until I was right next to Dad.

I was just about to drape it round his head when his eyes shot open. "Don't even think about it!" he hissed, making me jump.

"Thought you were asleep," I said.

"Obviously," he said. "And whatever that disgusting stuff is, put it back where you found it then turn over and go to sleep."

"I can't!" I complained. "I've been trying."

"Well, try harder," he said. "I don't want to hear another word from you until morning."

Fed up, I turned over the other way. If only I could get over to Derek Dobbs and put the cobwebs all over him! In the dark, I strained to see if I could see him. I wasn't even sure what group he was in, and everything – the whole room – was in total darkness now. All I could hear was lots of heavy breathing and snoring, some tick-tocks from a big old grandfather clock and the occasional click from one of the machines.

Reluctantly, I put the cobwebs back in their box, then squeezed my eyes shut and counted to a thousand.

I was still awake. The grandfather clock chimed two o'clock: two in the morning! I'd never been awake at that time before. I tried to play I Spy with myself but it didn't work.

The clock struck half past two. And then ... then ... just at the top of the stairs I saw a funny thing. A blob of light, a faint shape, shimmering and swaying.

I couldn't believe it! I nearly did a real girlie scream. I leaned over and shook Dad in his sleeping bag. "Quick!" I said. "A ghost!"

"Go back to sleep," he muttered.

"No, Dad! Really! There's a funny thing on the stairs. Quick! Look!"

Dad spoke in his crossest voice, through gritted teeth. "Dez," he said, "any more of your foolery and we'll just get up and go home. Now shut up and go ... to ... sleep!"

I shut up. Well, what else could I do with Dad about to go into one?

I stared as the blob turned into the shape of a person. It was a girl wearing a long white dress. She had lots of dark curls and a sparkly thing on her head. Her dress and everything else was faint and see-through, but I could see her face quite clearly.

"It's the bride!" I whispered in fright, but all that came from Dad was a snore. Then, just as I was going to shuffle over and tell the ghost hunters about it, the patch of misty light shimmered and moved, floating up the stairs again and away along the corridor.

I couldn't believe it! I'd seen a ghost.
Actually, really, seen a ghost. I tried to wake
Dad again but he wouldn't let me, so in the
end I didn't bother. I just lay there, all jittery
and too excited to sleep a wink. I remember
the clock striking three, then half past, and
after that I must have fallen asleep because I
couldn't remember any more until it was
morning and Miss Brown was bringing round
a big tray piled with bacon sandwiches.

Chapter Seven

"I saw a ghost!" was the first thing I said when I woke up.

"Sure you did," Dad said. "Had its head under its arm, did it?"

"No, honest! It was surrounded by a funny misty light and it floated on the stairs."

Miss Brown gave us a bacon sandwich each on a paper plate and Dad smiled at her smarmily. "You look bright-eyed and bushy-tailed this morning," he said.

"I don't know about that," Miss Brown said. "I'm sure I didn't sleep a wink."

Dad put down his sandwich and jumped out of his sleeping bag. "Miss Brown, do allow me to carry that heavy tray round for you."

"No, really, I'm fine," Miss Brown said.

"But Miss Brown…" Dad began.

"Mr Williams," Miss Brown said in a low voice, "I should tell you that although the children call me Miss Brown, I am in fact, Mrs Brown."

Dad looked taken aback at this. Almost shocked. To help him out I said, "I saw a ghost, Miss Brown!"

"Well, one hasn't been recorded on the calibration equipment," she said. "So it must have just appeared to you personally, Dez."

"It did! It did!"

"That's enough, Dez," Dad said gruffly. He sat down again. "Get on with your bacon sandwich."

"But I did see it!"

"You were dreaming," said Dad.

"No, I wasn't!"

But a bit later the ghost hunters confirmed that nothing strange or spooky had been recorded on their machines, so I didn't even bother to try and tell them. I knew what I'd seen, though. And I hadn't dreamed it.

After we'd eaten our sandwiches we wrote up some more stuff in our journals, then tidied up and collected all our gear. When we were on our way out, I happened to look up at the portraits on the stairs. There were all the usual sloppy-looking men with wigs, and then at the bottom, there was a painting of a girl wearing a long white dress and carrying flowers. My bride. Exactly as I'd seen her, with dark curls and the sparkly thing on her head.

"Look!" I tugged at Dad's tracksuit arm. "There's the ghost I saw!"

"Yes, yes," he said, then he said grumpily, "I think you could have told me that Miss Brown was married."

"I didn't know!" I said. "Anyway – look at that picture. It's my ghost. It is!"

"Look, Dez," Dad said firmly, "If that's the person you dreamed of, it's because you must have seen the portrait last night and somehow remembered it." He looked at me and frowned. "I do hope Miss Brown didn't think I was trying to ... well, you know ... be over-friendly towards her."

"I didn't dream it!"

"...Because that was the last thing I meant."

He scowled at me. "This whole trip has been a disaster and I can't help thinking that you're to blame. If Miss Brown hadn't been so miffed with you she..."

I didn't bother to listen to any more after that. He just went on and on about Miss Blooming Brown all the way home, and so I shut up about what I'd seen. There just wouldn't have been any point.

One thing had changed, though: I do believe in ghosts...